Jobs for Some People

Written by Brylee Gibson

Some people
have jobs like this.

But some people have jobs like this!

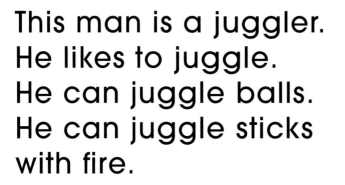

This man is a juggler.
He likes to juggle.
He can juggle balls.
He can juggle sticks
with fire.

This man is a magician.
Look at his hat.
A rabbit is inside his hat.
He can make the rabbit
come out.

This man is a dancer.
He likes to dance.
He can spin on his back.
He can spin on his hands.

8

This woman is a drummer.
She can play the drums
with her hands.
She can play the drums
with her feet, too.

This woman is a clown.
She can make a hat
with a balloon.
She can make
the children laugh.

This man has puppets.
He can make
the puppets walk.
He can make
the puppets dance.

Index

Guide Notes

Title: **Jobs for Some People**
Stage: Early (2) – Yellow

Genre: Nonfiction
Approach: Guided Reading
Processes: Thinking Critically, Exploring Language, Processing Information
Written and Visual Focus: Photographs (static images), Index, Labels
Word Count: 134

THINKING CRITICALLY
(sample questions)
- Look at the title and read it to the children. Ask the children what they know about different jobs that people can do.
- Focus the children's attention on the index. Ask: "What are you going to find out about in this book?"
- If you want to find out about a juggler, which page would you look on?
- If you want to find out about a dancer, which page would you look on?
- Look at pages 14 and 15. Why do you think some people might like to have a job like this?
- How do you think some of the people might learn to do the jobs mentioned in this book ?

EXPLORING LANGUAGE

Terminology
Title, cover, photographs, author, photographers

Vocabulary
Interest words: juggler, juggle, magician, dancer, spin, drummer, drums, puppets
High-frequency words: make, her
Positional words: on, out

Print Conventions
Capital letter for sentence beginnings, periods, comma, exclamation mark